When I grow up, I'm going to play for ... SCOTLAND

Written by Gemma Cary
Illustrated by Tatio Viana and Adrian Bijloo
Designed by Sarah Allen

First published by Hometown World in 2015
Hometown World Ltd
7 Northumberland Buildings
Bath BA1 2JB

www.hometownworld.co.uk

ISBN 978-1-84993-970-6
Printed in China

10 9 8 7 6 5 4 3 2 1

When I grow up, I'm going to play for ...
SCOTLAND

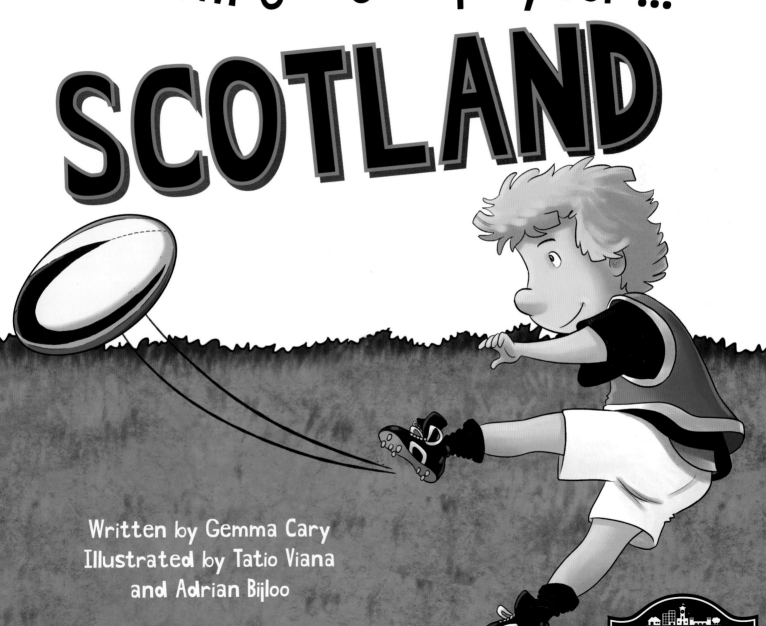

Written by Gemma Cary
Illustrated by Tatio Viana
and Adrian Bijloo

CHILDHOOD DREAMS
HOMETOWN WORLD

"**Out you go,**" said Mum, and the screen went black.

"**No!**" wailed Jack.

"**I was twelve-nil up!**"
"Very good," said Mum. "Now go and play outside."
Jack glanced at the window and saw their cat, Furball, scowling in the rain.
"**But ...**"

Soon Jack found himself outside, standing in a puddle. What was he meant to do out here? His rugby ball was flat and there was no one to play with.

On the back of his bedroom door, Jack found what he wanted: his **Scotland shirt.**

For some reason, he always felt more confident wearing this shirt, and he usually played better too. He put it on and instantly felt happier.

Back outside, it had stopped raining. Jack grabbed a frizzy tennis ball in both hands and practised his passing.

He kicked the ball through the defensive washing line, like his heroes from the Scotland team.

He scooped up the ball, dodged around the flower beds, then dived to the ground, scoring a terrific try.

Jack celebrated with a big kick into the crowd but ... the ball sailed right over the fence and hit something with a satisfying

thwack.

"Owww!"

squealed old Mrs Bettershed,
who had been busy digging up carrots.
"My bottom!"

Just then, Jack heard the familiar thump of a car door.

"Hello, Mrs Bettershed," called Jack's dad, appearing in the back garden. Mrs Bettershed glowered and speared the tennis ball with her hefty pitchfork. "Sorry," said Jack, trying not to laugh.

"Hello, Superstar!" Dad said to Jack. "I've bought us a present."

Dad held out a bag and Jack peered inside. It was a brand-new rugby ball! Not only that – it was in the colours of their favourite team, **Scotland.**

Whooooosh!

The pair were soon having their best-ever
game of rugby. They seemed to play for hours!
When they eventually stopped for tea, Dad said,
"I've spoken to our local team and they're having a trial
tomorrow. They said you can come along, if you want to."

Next day, father and son arrived at the rugby ground ... The changing rooms bustled with children in blue and red bibs, nervously waiting to show off their skills.

The coach soon signalled for Jack to join a game and Jack raced over. He cheered when others made good breaks and encouraged players who missed conversions. When one boy fell over, Jack helped him up.

But secretly, Jack was worried about his own performance. When the half-time whistle blew, he had barely touched the ball, let alone scored a try.

Someone near the subs' bench caught Jack's eye. It was his dad, waving madly. Jack jogged over and his dad pulled the Scotland shirt from a rucksack.

"Wear this under your bib, Son. You always play brilliantly with this on."

Jack did as his dad said. As he sprinted back onto the field, he imagined he was stepping out of the tunnel at Murrayfield. Blue and white banners rippled in the air while the crowd sang the national anthem.

All of a sudden, Jack was the best player on the field! In the second half he scored three incredible tries, while no one else scored more than one.
He was confident. He was happy. He was ...

At the end of the trial, the coach called out the names of players who had made the final fifteen: "Danny, Olly, Leo, Lucas ..."

Everyone clapped after each name.

"Lewis, Noah, Sam, Josh, Max, Ethan ..."

"Waaahoooo!"

Jack leapt into the air, waving his arms
in excitement.
"I'll take that as a 'yes'," said the
coach, and everyone laughed.

Dad couldn't stop grinning. He praised Jack all the way home. "You were amazing, Son! Unstoppable. A real champion!"

"Cheers, Dad," Jack replied. "I can't wait for my first match. But one day I suppose I won't be able to play for them any more."

"Oh? Why not?" asked Dad.

"Because when I grow up, I'm going to play for Scotland!"

And guess who else is going to play for Scotland?

You are!

SCOTLAND'S NEXT SUPERSTAR!

Write your name here

Thomas Hamilton

Stick your photo here

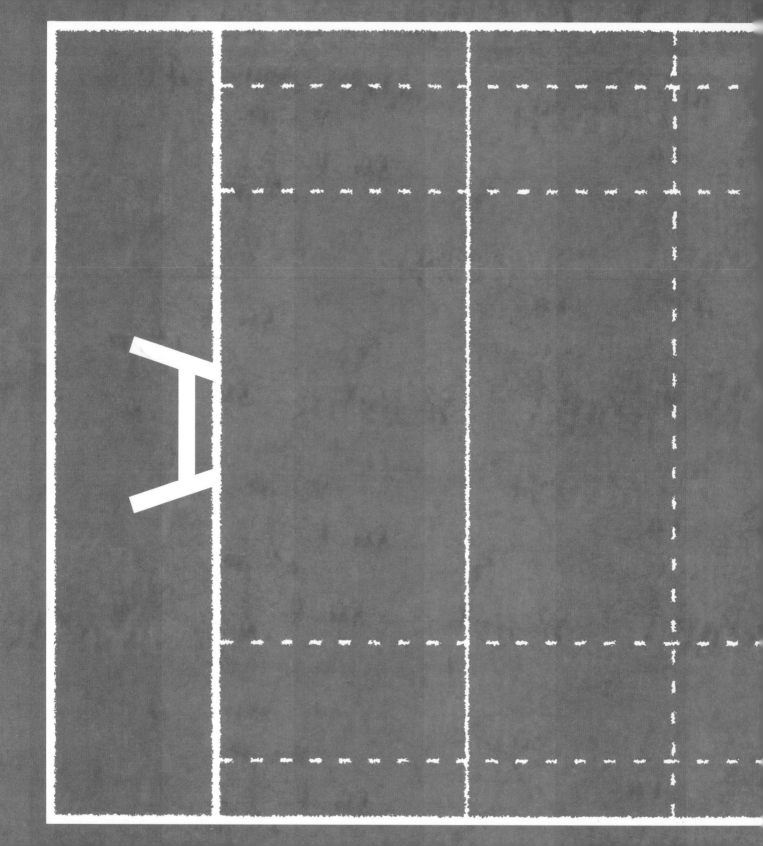